HAROLD MEEK

HORN AND CONDUCTOR
Reminiscences of a Practitioner
with a Few Words of Advice

HAROLD MEEK

HORN AND CONDUCTOR

Reminiscences of a Practitioner
with a Few Words of Advice

Foreword by Alfred Mann

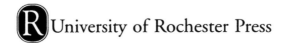

University of Rochester Press

First published 1997

University of Rochester Press
34–36 Administration Building
University of Rochester
Rochester, NY 14627   USA

and at P.O. Box 9
Woodbridge, Suffolk IP12 3DF
United Kingdom

ISBN 1–878822–83–7 (Paperback)

Library of Congress Cataloging-in-Publication Data
Meek, Harold L.
    Horn and conductor : reminiscences of a practitioner with a
few words of advice / Harold Meek ; foreword by Alfred Mann.
        p.   cm.
    Includes bibliographical references (p. 117)
    ISBN 1–878822–83–7
    1. Meek, Harold L.   2. Horn players—United States—
Biography.   3. Orchestral musicians—Anecdotes.   4. Conductors (Music)—Anecdotes.   I. Mann, Alfred.   II. Title.
ML419.M44A3   1997
788.9′4—dc20   96-44230
                                                                                      CIP
                                                                                      MN

British Library Cataloguing-in-Publication Data
A catalogue record for this book is
available from the British Library

Designed and typeset by Cornerstone Composition Services
Printed in the United States of America
This publication is printed on acid-free paper

To the Memory
of my Father and Mother

CONTENTS

ACKNOWLEDGMENTS

Much is owed to my friends and colleagues who contributed, each in his or her own way, to the researching and writing of this project: to Alexander J. Grieve OAM for the letter and photographs Dennis Brain sent to his brother, Gordon Grieve; to Osbourne McConathy and Robert Renton for anecdotes about some of the *maestri* herein; to Mary Fransden for research on my behalf in the Sibley Music Library, locating scores for nearly 100 works and over 1,800 recordings, which I sifted through and studied during several trips to Rochester; to Mary Davidson, chief librarian at Sibley and her staff, especially for the attention the staff gave me in the recorded music listening facility; to Diane Ota, chief of the music division, and staff of the Boston Public Library, for their assistance and courtesies, and to John Bergstrom for his fine work on the music examples.

Professor Hans Pizka, Munich, and Professor Friedrich Gabler, Vienna added valuable material about the Vienna Horn; James and Peggy Allen Brink read the manuscript, as it progressed, and typed it. Martin Bookspan made critical evaluations which are greatly appreciated. W. Peter Kurau guided my speech patterns here and there to academic politeness.

Finally, to Alfred Mann I owe deep gratitude for his sympathetic editing of the final manuscript, and also Robert Freeman, who suggested the project and encouraged it through to its completion.

Harold Meek, Boston 1996

FOREWORD

The heroic age of the symphony and its time-honored institutions is fading. Yesterday's grand gestures, such as the founding of the NBC Symphony Orchestra to provide Toscanini with his personal ensemble, or the establishment of the "Amsterdam Strings" which allowed New York's radio station WNYC to offer its own live programs conducted by Klemperer, have no counterpart today.

The changing world of maestro and performer is in this little volume the subject of one who lived through the transition and whose distinguished career reflects both the front rank and front lines of Philharmonic battles and guerrillas, of the glory and the problems of orchestral magic. The young protegé of Reiner and Koussevitzky, the keen observer of Stokowski's and Szell's charisma, speaks here from the perspective of their and his daily workshop, from the encounters, joys and intricacies of their glamorous and at times controversial association.

It is the account of an epoch whose impact needs to be preserved. Though seemingly under dictatorial rule, the performing artist experienced a freedom essential to artistic expression. The symphony orchestra is a strangely "un-modern" phenomenon which, by its very nature, resists democratization as it resists mechanization. The single musician's vision may, in given circumstances, prove superior to that of the orchestra's leader. And the judgment of individual orchestra members is discerning in a way the machine is not, although the ideal of absolute perfection has begun to threaten that of spontaneous expression. The "perfect" ensemble's secret is invariably founded in the rapport of player and conductor.

One of the author's great regrets is that this rapport has, in time, lost much of its personal quality, and the anecdotes woven through his account are apt to produce nostalgia in our time. But they are more than anecdotes; they are part of a culture as well as a social picture. The personal basis stood for more than a degree of mere acquaintance.

One wonders at the characterization of mid-century leading conductors. Has artistic communication changed that much? What has clearly changed is the attitude toward the musical work. We are no longer prone to think in such terms as "Toscanini's Beethoven Symphonies" or "Bruno Walter's Mozart." And it is interesting, though futile, to consider the loss or the gain.

It is of value to the specialist as well as the general reader to go through the symphonic excerpts chosen from the point of view of the horn player with detailed references to the interpretation of great conductors. The history of the horn is treated elsewhere more extensively, but one is apt to find the name of this exponent of the instrument in the best of it.

The author had made his mark early in the orchestral world. When Fritz Reiner came to the Boston Symphony Orchestra as a guest conductor, the orchestra members, aware of his well-known disposition, were wondering what ill-mooded charge might come forth as a greeting. Yet Reiner, peering over his glasses, fastened his sour look on a young one among them, possibly the youngest of the players—to whom he had once given the fare to travel back from the conductor's home in Westport, Connecticut—and the weighty opening message proved to be: "Mr. Meek, I presume?"

Alfred Mann
Eastman School of Music
University of Rochester

INTRODUCTION

The horn, the horn, the lusty horn
is not a thing to laugh to scorn.
Shakespeare, *As You Like It*, Act IV

The horn which today's conductor encounters, lusty or not, is the product and culmination of a history spanning many centuries. It is an instrument which can evoke utmost tenderness and pathos, eerie pianissimi, singing lyrical phrases, as well as the bright signal—lusty indeed—of Siegfried's call in Wagner's *Ring*. The conductor's challenge is to guide and control the wealth of the instrument's expression, the instrument's "instrument" being, of course, a skillful player. The baton emits no sound.

. . . there is one chief problem which occupies the conductor in all contexts: the treatment of brass and percussion and, in particular, of natural instruments and kettle drums in forte passages of classic music. According to the intentions of classical composers, the forte of natural horns and trumpets is meant to give vigor and brilliance to that of the whole orchestra, and it is the task of the conductor to fulfill this demand without disturbing or encumbering the main melodic line of strings or woodwinds by the volume of non-melodic notes. The composers have made this difficult for us, and even Mozart, that profound connoisseur of the orchestra and master of orchestration has, by his summary forte directions for trumpets, horns and kettle drums in energetic passages, posed a difficult task to the aural sense of the conductor and his endeavors for clarity . . ."[1]

Having served my years as a horn player in various orchestras, I have met with some conductors who held the opinion that, simply because the horn is a brass instrument, it will and should sound as strong as the trombone. More than once have I gone to a conductor in his Green Room to point out that we just cannot compete dynamically with the trombone. Should he want the volume of a trombone, then by all means he should re-score the passage in question.

Many years ago, Anton Horner, the great first horn player of the Philadelphia Orchestra—how rightly was he named!—stood up during a rehearsal and told Fritz Reiner that the lips of the horn players could not stand the pressure to which he was subjecting them in demanding more and more forte. Later he went to Reiner, grabbed his thumb and squeezed it between his own thumb and forefinger until it turned red and blue, saying, "This is what happens to us—circulation is cut off, and the lips become numb." The maestro rubbed his thumb and understood.

After many seasons in the vineyard of the brass section, it occurred to me that I might share my experiences with younger colleagues and their interested fellow readers because an era of great conductors—and great horn players—begins to sink into the past as our century draws to a close. Great advances have been made on many fronts. Technology and the CD are there to "record" them for posterity. But the statement of the eye-witness retains its special place. His eye (and ear) can make a contribution, whatever authority they may be allowed; his memory can help, at times amuse, and above all give evidence.

---

[1]Bruno Walter. *Of Music and Music Making*. New York: W. W. Norton, 1961, 134.

Speaking of recordings, I have to make a personal confession. I have never heard as many "technically" flawed performances on LP, tapes or old wax platters in sixty years, as I have in two years of compact discs. The great merits of the CD are beyond dispute. But we are apt to think that they have solved all problems. They have not—they may be more "perfect" than actual concert performances, but we are left to question: "What does that really mean?" There are two sides to the story.

True, recording on wax platters had its obvious dangers, not the least of which was the tension felt by artists during the recording session. One "slip," and an entire segment had to be done over. And once the slip was made, tension mounted all the more as each player became concerned about possibly making the next. Another, though only occasional problem was that the stylus cutting the wax master would not discard its fine ribbon of cut wax, which marred the grooves already cut. Still another cause for the loss of a day's recording efforts—with the prospect of beginning all over again the next morning—occurred in Tanglewood when part of the Boston Symphony's wind section was making a wax recording in the Opera-Concert Hall with Koussevitzky. We began on a hot afternoon in July to record Mozart's Serenade in E flat, K 361, for thirteen wind instruments. The stage was stifling, gradually becoming worse as the sun rose to its zenith. Finally, it became so hot that the engineer turned out the red recording lamp. "The wax has melted and we cannot continue." But we returned in the cool of the next morning and the wax performed admirably, producing an unforgettable recording!

I readily admit the immense progress of modern engineering replacing wild adventure—and wild it often was. I might quote the afterlude of Van Cliburn's performance of the Tchaikovsky B flat Minor Piano Concerto with Munch and the Boston Symphony. Rumors of a possible recording session had been on, then off, then on again, then off again for six days. We played a final concert on Sunday afternoon, beginning at three o'clock, going home around five and expecting that that was the end of a grueling seven days' work. Not so. About eight p.m. the symphony staff began telephoning every member of the orchestra to come to Symphony Hall at midnight to begin a recording session. Everyone was there at midnight, waiting to begin. At least fifteen minutes went by before Munch and Cliburn came onstage. The gossip going the rounds of the orchestra while we waited was that Cliburn was praying in the Green Room before undertaking his work. We had heard that this was his routine before every concert and wondered if Munch was praying too.

The session finally began with RCA Victor's costs running from midnight onward. We had completed one work when Cliburn decided to try another, the Schumann Concerto. We stayed until five a.m. when victory was declared. (The story had an unhappy ending, because neither recording was ever released.)

Munch, concerned only with the quality of the recording, had remained calm as usual—everything was being put on tape by this time, and a good recording could be spliced together. Richard Mohr, then RCA's producer for the Boston Symphony recordings, related the characteristic story of a well-known Metropolitan Opera soprano who frequently came to RCA's New York studio to sing a high C, D, E, or F when she was in good voice. The notes were then placed in her "file" to be used as needed.

In distinction to Munch, Koussevitzky, prey to the old-fashioned system, was always tense. His final words to the recording engineer before the red recording lamp glowed onstage were invariably, "Don't touch the *apparat*"—meaning: I want the dynamics to be *mine*.

It is no secret that in modern recordings the dynamics—when all the editing is done—remain the engineers'. As a rule, highly capable and knowledgeable, they are concerned only with the perfection of the recording. As a result, many a concert-goer has been disappointed upon hearing a live performance by performers famed for their recordings. But what shall we say about the immeasurable loss of the electrifying "live" impression in the well-equipped audio set-up of the modern home?

Because, to a large extent, the enjoyment of symphonic music has moved from the concert hall to the home, its audience will have to face the fact that it is dealing with a triangular team: performer, conductor, and engineer. There was a time when the team consisted of only two agents: performer and conductor—to which our discussion shall be devoted.

Many conductors, including Bruno Walter, have assumed that the piano should be their instrument, and stringed and wind instruments might serve them only by way of collateral general acquaintance. I do not agree. It seems a better situation to me—despite the incontestably primary role of the piano—when the conductor evolves from the orchestra itself. Pierre Monteux, Charles Munch, Serge Koussevitzky, Bernard Haitink, Klaus Tennstedt, and Frederick Stock all played in orchestras before becoming conductors. Vladimir Golschmann studied horn for a time with Edward Murphy, the long-time first horn player of the St. Louis Symphony. There is a tremendous advantage in the conductor's first-hand acquaintance with what it is like to sit in an orchestra. Fine points are known and understood, and thus can be called for.

SOME FINE POINTS

Balancing natural dynamics is one of them. Virgil Thomson's statement, made at mid-century, gives pause for thought:

> Notable as a characteristic of contemporary American orchestral styles is the systematic employment of forced tone, of overbowing and overblowing.[2]

This applies in a particular way to the horn section. It is sad to report that many conductors think of the horn section as consisting of a first horn and "the others." Nothing is further from the truth. Each part is a specialty unto itself.

> "[The American] habit of constantly showing off the wind instrument soloists makes for an impoverishment of sound that is peculiarly American.
>
> A passage for three clarinets, oboes, or bassoons, for instance, always sounds like a solo for the first desk, the other parts constituting merely a more or less harmonious shadow. And we almost never achieve the equilibrium in trumpet, horn, or trombone chords that is characteristic of even the most routine French playing.
>
> We allow our first flute, oboe, first trumpet, horn or trombone to dominate colleagues simply because he is usually a more accomplished player and able to produce by legitimate means a larger tone. All this adds to the decibel count, though not necessarily to richness of effect.[3]

---

[2] *The Art of Judging Music.* New York: Alfred A. Knopf, 1947, p. 230.
[3] *Ibid.*

Just as in a vocal quartet there are different ranges and qualities within the given ranges, so it is in the horn section. The high horns do best in their range, although they can sound the lowest notes as well. The low horns tend to have a better quality in their range, although they again can play in a higher tessitura. Some tenors can sing in the baritone range, but that does not mean that they sound well there. This is true also for the horn. Tone quality is the deciding factor.

One of England's fine horn players, Patrick Strevens, who has played in the London Philharmonic and Royal Opera House, wrote an article for a specialized periodical, then newly established, and we might quote from it in some pertinent detail:

> I make no apology for ensuring that our new journal puts the spotlight on that unsung hero, the fourth horn. It has even been said that one of our former British orchestra makers coined the phrase, 'Find me a good fourth and I'll build you a good horn quartet.' The purpose of the fourth horn is to provide a firm foundation for the rest of the quartet. However good the upper three players, they cannot possibly play in tune if there is the slightest wavering of the bass line; and intonation and tone are so clearly linked that players normally capable of the creamiest tone sound dull and ordinary if the section's tuning is suspect. This may seem a fairly obvious point to make, but there are some first and third players, to say nothing of teachers, who either fail to appreciate these factors or have some vague notion of their influence but have never put it into words. . . . Take a careful look at the seating of the quartet. Many conductors and first horns prefer to have their sections strung out in a line, and I am only too well aware of the advantages of this system. But let us look at the hidden advantages of sitting three in front (I am assuming the first horn has a 'bumper-up' [assistant]) and two behind. This way, number four is in close touch with number one's dynamics. This in itself is a great help, but there is also a feed-back in quartet playing because the first

horn can hear the bass notes of the section's harmony more closely.[4]

Erich Leinsdorf tried this system in Boston, and there are distinct advantages to it. We also tried wooden reflectors or baffles at one point for Munch, when James Stagliano and I remained after a rehearsal to test the idea. The point was to try to keep the horn sound from getting lost in that of the trombones and tympani. Georg Boettcher, first horn in Boston 1928-36, however, had a seating plan, I believe the best of any, which I have used many times in ensembles other than the Boston Symphony. It is the "line" formation in reverse order: the first horn sits where the fourth horn would normally be, followed to the left by the second, third, and fourth. The first can hear the section clearly and himself or herself better because the bell is not obstructed by another horn and person.

I once had a conductor tell me to arrange the players to suit myself. That would have meant open warfare among the section. Players cannot hear themselves as the conductor can, so this remains a doubly poor proposition.

When I played first horn in the Rochester Philharmonic Orchestra, José Iturbi, the great pianist who was then conductor of that orchestra, said to me a good many times, "Mr. Milk, please, a different tone." How wonderful it would have been had he been able to put into words what he wanted! Fritz Reiner was more articulate in formulating his wishes for a given instrument. A taskmaster, sarcastic and autocratic—but miraculously able to make great music!

*   *   *

Another aspect of interpreting the score comes with the knowledge of articulation. Only a few conductors with whom I have

---

[4]"The Horn Call," *Journal of the International Horn Society,* Vol. 1, No. 1, February 1971.

come in contact really understand this. Articulation is important not only for individual instruments, but also in the sense that, when called for by the composer for the entire orchestra, it sounds the same from each section. And if written in a continuous phrase, it must be the identical sameness all the way through—not just for a few beginning notes. Conductors are apt to be careless in this regard. Good ensemble is expected of the horns, as it is of all sections of the orchestra. It can be helped by a clear beat from the conductor's baton. Listening to each other is not always enough.

Intonation is the problem and province of the player, but here again a sympathetic conductor can help an occasional lapse by subtly signalling the errant horn player. As we play, the instrument gets warmer from our breath, and the overall pitch tends to rise. While we try to compensate for this, the conductor should understand the fact and be alert to it.

The music director of an orchestra should, above all, be aware of the fact that different horn players, like different singers, have essentially a bright or a dark tone, and that the musicianship of the individual will determine the blend with the ensemble—not the manufacture or style of the instrument. Dennis Brain, the great British horn player who set the standard for all the horn soloists to follow, said, "The sound a horn player produces is foremost the physical make-up of the individual player."

Some conductors believe that if all players in a horn section use instruments from the same manufacturer, a homogeneous sound will result. However, a blindfold test given in 1971 at a seminar of the International Horn Society at Pomona College, Claremont, California, proved that this is not the case. Three distinguished horn soloists: Barry Tuckwell, Ralph Pyle, and James Decker played various manufacturers' instruments for a blindfolded panel. The overriding result was that a player sounds the same no matter what horn is being used.

Yet people may think that what they see is what they hear. Christoph von Dohnányí, conductor of the Cleveland Orchestra, made his incoming horn players change to the instrument he considered to produce the ideal sound. I understand that he no longer follows this practice. Yet I once sat with Guido Cantelli, Toscanini's heir-apparent at the NBC Symphony Orchestra, on a train ride from New London, Connecticut to New York for concerts which he was to conduct. He informed me that the best horn in America was a Conn 8-D. His experiences with American orchestras was still very limited, and thus he knew necessarily little about horns in America. The first horn player of the NBC Symphony, Arthur Berv, had used that particular make of instrument, and other players in that section used the same make. But what caused them to blend well was their musicianship. Would a conductor insist that all violin players in his orchestra play only Stradivari instruments? I am not so sure that homogeneity is the thing to strive for in the first place. If that is the goal, perhaps an organ transcription would be the best solution.

THE APPLICANT

The way in which a horn player joins an orchestra has greatly changed in the course of our century. In the summers of 1941 and 1942 I was a fellowship student at the Berkshire Music Center. Koussevitzky had seen his dream come true: a school where talented young musicians could work exhaustively with the best teachers in surroundings of great beauty. The summer of 1942 was different in that the student orchestra worked every day except Monday for the five-week season, preparing public concerts. The Boston Symphony Orchestra was not in residence that year because its trustees had cancelled their Festival due to the war. I was fortunate to play first horn most of the time, and so came under close scrutiny of Koussevitzky. When the season ended, I was invited to his home, Seranak, overlooking Stockbridge Bowl. As I walked up its long driveway, I was joined by Mario Lanza who, it turned out, had an appointment just after mine. He was in school that year too, and was hailed as the next Caruso. We were both to have our careers launched that morning and to receive the blessing of our mentor.

Koussevitzky had earlier extended an invitation for me to join his orchestra in the fall, but his trustees would not pay for another player that year. However, when we met, he said, "Don't vorry for vee vill be together. But how vould you like it to go to Pittsburgh now? Reiner is looking for a horn and I vill call him." He went to the phone and asked the operator for Reiner's number. It turned out to be unlisted, and the operator refused to give it to him. No amount of entreating and saying, "But I am Serge Koussevitzky" would do. So he promised to write, and in due time I received a letter from Reiner inviting me to his summer home in Westport, Connecticut, for an audition. Auditions were indeed heard by conductors, not by committees, as is the custom today. I was accepted by Reiner for the season 1942-43 and offered a contract which was to be mailed by his manager to my home in Newark, Ohio. During the audition I played, among other things, Mendelssohn's Nocturne from *A Midsummer Night's Dream*. Reiner showed me his phrasing, which differs from Mendelssohn's but makes good sense. Through the breath after the half note in the fourth full bar, the quarter note becomes the upbeat for the next phrase, just as the very first upbeat begins the entire piece. Here is a case where the conductor may be said to have refined on the composer's indications.

I had brought along two different instruments for the audition: one a brass horn with normal bore and bell, producing a lovely clear, ringing sound; the other a heavier, wide-bore horn made of silver. He liked the idea of using different instruments for different repertoire: for example, the brass horn for the Nocturne, the heavier horn for Siegfried's call—something that was not in vogue in 1942 as it is in today's orchestra.

Reiner gave me the return train fare to my home—music students were as poor then as always, though I cannot imagine such a thing happening today.

On the return journey from Westport to my home, I took a detour to stop off in Rochester, New York, and see friends at the Eastman School of Music to tell them of my good fortune. No sooner had I gotten inside the door when several people rushed toward me saying, "Brouk has just resigned, and the first horn position here is open. If you want it, see Harrison and arrange to play for him."

Frank Brouk had come from the Chicago Symphony to fill the vacancy when Fred Klein had accepted the first horn position in the newly-created Columbia Broadcasting Orchestra which Bruno Walter conducted. Guy Fraser Harrison was the long-time conductor of the Rochester Civic Orchestra. In only a few minutes, Harrison came into the Eastman Theater, and I unpacked and played. While still a student at Eastman, I had substituted a few times for Klein when he was indisposed, so Harrison and I were not strangers to one another. I got the job, improved on the financial offer from Reiner, and signed a contract then and there.

In early 1943 I had a long distance call during a rehearsal from Bruno Zirato, manager of the New York Philharmonic. Our manager, Arthur See, interrupted Harrison and, I suppose, told him what was happening; I was excused to take the call. Mr. Zirato told me that Bruno Jaenicke, their world-famous first horn player, had suffered a heart attack, and would I come to New York to finish the season in his place. I was utterly amazed and somewhat awed by this offer, as well as shocked at the bad news about Jaenicke. "How did they know about me?" I asked. I was young, with no reputation yet, and was just then getting started in the professional world. Zirato's answer was that Koussevitzky had recommended me. When I told Mr. Zirato that I was under contract to Rochester, he said he had not been told that, but would I be interested in the full-time opening for the position at the beginning of the next season (1943-44)? If so, would I play for Arthur Rodzinski in Cleveland? Of course I was interested and made arrangements for an audition. Rodzinski was to be the new conductor of the New York Philharmonic. My playing went well and I was offered the position, but I did not sign a contract at that point.

A very short time after returning to Rochester, I received a telegram from Koussevitzky offering me the first horn position in the second quartet and the third horn position in the first quartet of the Boston Symphony Orchestra. Salary was quoted. It did not take me long to make up my mind, and in short order I accepted the offer. I never regretted that decision. Boston was a much better ensemble at that time, and the city had a better quality of life than New York could offer. It was not until three years later that I learned the circumstances behind the recommendation: Koussevitzky had threatened to leave the Boston Symphony and go to the New York Philharmonic as its conductor, and he wanted me to go with him as his first horn. What a person to have behind a young musician at the beginning of his long professional journey! I entered the Boston Symphony with a three-year contract and high hopes, high hopes that were to be fulfilled.

What great advantage that conductor and instrumentalist could meet at the outset—would that today's candidates could find a similarly direct road to their working association!

*   *   *

Koussevitzky's retirement announcement in early 1948 carried with it notice of non-renewal of contract for eight members of the orchestra, the maximum number under our Trade Agreement for any one season. Koussevitzky said that he had had no part of it, and I believed him. Why, in his last moments with this orchestra, would he have any reason to change personnel for which he was no longer responsible?

At the time I was a member of the Committee on Dismissals and Non-Renewals in the orchestra. During the Pops season, which began in May, I went to see Henry Cabot, president of the orchestra's trustees, a man of great integrity, one who always had the best interests of the orchestra in mind; I knew he did not take his position lightly. Once I had broached the subject, he began by saying that the trustees would never again give so much power to a conductor as they had given to Koussevitzky. Koussevitzky, so to speak, had power of life and death over the members of the Boston Symphony—although he had built it lovingly and had had the greatest personal pride in it. He felt like a father to this group of one hundred and ten orchestra members and would sometimes address them as "Kinder."

To my great surprise, Cabot said that he himself took the responsibility for the pink slips. I remember that I stammered, "Why did you take this upon yourself, Mr. Cabot? You are not a musician." He must have thought this an impertinence though he did not show it. I had always gotten along well with Henry Cabot and had held him in high esteem. Several times I had gone to him in matters concerning my own contract, and he had once said, "It is fellows like you that we have to take care of." Perhaps that helped me at this moment. In any event, the discussion continued, and in the end Cabot promised to ask the incoming conductor, Charles Munch, to audition the people concerned and then to follow his decisions in the matter. (Koussevitzky had recommended to the Trustees that they take his protegé, Leonard Bernstein, to be his successor, but the Trustees would have none of it.)

The Committee on Dismissals and Non-Renewals did approach Munch when he arrived in Boston, and he agreed to listen to each of the eight men. But there was a caveat. He agreed only if we five members of the Committee were present in the Green Room to hear our colleagues play. Fortunately, there were two French members on the Committee who could communicate with Munch in his own language so that he understood our intentions and we understood his. The auditions were agony for us of the committee and for our colleagues. Several had been in the orchestra for twenty years or longer. I was embarrassed for them all. To our relief, all but one were reinstated in the orchestra for at least a year, and two were to remain thirty years longer.

*   *   *

This experience, however, led to something worse, something which today has become the norm for auditions in all American orchestras: audition by committee. There are those who see only something benign in the committee process. But it is unwieldy, puts everyone under enormous pressure, and it is totally unfair to expect that players fly from East to West and vice versa, getting off planes and playing for a group which, at that moment, can say "yes" or "no, you cannot play for the conductor." They are apt to be wrong part of the time. After eight or ten people have played, the committee members often do not know who played what, or how. If conductors have no time to take full charge and care for this part of their responsibilities, perhaps orchestra trustees should begin to look for conductors who do.

When I was a fifteen-year-old student in Pittsburgh, my horn teacher, August Fischer, advised me to play an audition for any conductor who would hear me. This was to be for the experience of a one-to-one meeting and its critical reaction from the conductor right on the spot. Otto Klemperer once listened to me backstage in Pittsburgh's Syria Mosque's auditorium. He was very kind and offered suggestions and advice when I played the horn solo from the second movement of Brahms' First Symphony. Young people today miss this experience. All music is poorer because of it. In the early days, a player could play for a conductor even if there were no vacancies at the moment and be told that they would be kept in mind and advised when one occurred; and most conductors kept their word.

*   *   *

The Boston Symphony members had never belonged to a union since the orchestra's beginnings in 1881, because Henry Higginson, its founder and financial backer, would brook no interference from any outside source, especially from a workers' union. The orchestra was to uphold the highest standards, and he felt that organized labor had no place in his plan. Consequently, the orchestra had remained without a union organization until February 1943, when its members joined the American Federation of Musicians.

The contract forms which were in use when I entered the orchestra in September 1943 strictly forbade any player from playing in any outside orchestra until the termination of his contract. Further, he could not play for any Balls. He could not play for any broadcasting or recording session without permission of the Corporation. As a matter of record, I have a contract dated 1954 which was still holding to these restrictions. In other words, one was bound to the Boston Symphony only.

The main reason the orchestra's trustees allowed the orchestra members to join the union was a very simple economic one: stage hands and electricians in some of the halls where the orchestra played while on tour would refuse to handle our baggage because of the orchestra's non-union status. Members furnished their own wardrobe trunks which the Corporation transported on tour along with music and the conductor's and management's baggage. Also, RCA, the orchestra's recording contractor, was becoming increasingly nervous regarding its relationship with the orchestra because of its non-union status. When I entered the first rehearsal in September 1943, the new rules of unionism were just beginning to make themselves felt. Under the old order, Koussevitzky could rehearse as long as he wanted. And I learned that rehearsals of four hours and more had not been uncommon. When I joined, they had just been limited to three hours, from ten in the morning until one o'clock in the afternoon. A large clock hung in the center of the back wall of the stage where the conductor could readily see it. One or two minutes over the allotted time were not unknown for the first few months, but as the season progressed and the custom of a few extra minutes did not cease, charges were made to the management as per the contract for overtime pay. Koussevitzky now began to pay close attention to the clock.

*   *   *

Players trained today are probably the best technically-equipped of all generations; however, in far too many cases, that is where it ends. They play everything mezzoforte, or forte, and everything fast, rushing from note to note with no feeling or expression. And conductors accept it as the norm. Why is this? The obvious answer is that conductors, too, are cut from the same cloth. Koussevitzky used to tell us that mezzoforte was the most "uninteresting dynamic kee exist." Any sense of the long line in music seems absent in too many performances today. I quote Bruno Walter on the subject: "There is many a conductor who considers perfect precision of performance the essential part of his task. It is no wonder that, in our age, dominated by technique as it is, the idea of mechanical perfection should have intruded into the realm of art, and that precision should have begun to be of overwhelming importance in the opinion of many circles."[5]

After Munch's first concert, many long-time patrons noted that this was not the Boston Symphony of great art which they had known, loved and supported for the past twenty-five years. What had been a highly dedicated, self-disciplined group of artists suddenly had become slack. Many of the old patrons gave up their seats in Symphony Hall and new faces began to appear. Munch would bring a new repertoire, with accent on the French composer, and a looseness in playing and stage deportment. He did not particularly like to rehearse, and often shortened rehearsals drastically. Sometimes he cancelled them altogether in advance, or telephoned from his house after we were already assembled onstage, to say that we could go home. This attitude affected morale, and it showed in the playing. Yet new audiences began to be built around this new figure, and the public began to accept as the norm this rather different Boston Symphony Orchestra.

---

[5]*Op. cit.*, p. 125.

THE AUTOCRAT

The reverse side of the close association between orchestra member and conductor, beginning with an audition in which the two of them faced each other alone, showed itself in the autocratic role the conductor maintained throughout.

Koussevitzky's demeanor was intense and controlling. There was absolutely no smoking (yes, smoking on stage before rehearsals and during intermissions was commonplace in orchestras at those times). The orchestra was tuned in the tuning room before entering the stage; there was no practicing on stage before Koussevitzky appeared and certainly no showing off, playing passages unrelated to the repertoire for that day. Dead silence prevailed on the stage when the side door opened and Koussevitzky walked to the podium. He was the sole authority. No one spoke; no one questioned anything. If anyone dared, he was either reprimanded then and there, or was requested to see Koussevitzky upstairs in his dressing room after the rehearsal. In earlier times, Koussevitzky sent a person from the stage if he was not pleased or thought he had noticed a lack of attention. He had, at times, made grown men cry.

Koussevitzky regarded Symphony Hall as "dee Temple," and one did not desecrate it. He also had a hand in deciding who or what else appeared within its hallowed walls besides His Orchestra. Certain groups not up to his standards were not allowed to perform there. (Spike Jones and his loony band had done a performance—unknown to Koussevitzky. Economics had been at the bottom of the trustees' decision to allow any kind of performance by anyone if they had the fee to pay, and this consideration was dropped.) Koussevitzky also decided whom to invite as guest conductor when he took his two-week mid-winter break. Yet he hardly ever left his orchestra in strange hands while he was off as a guest conductor. His job was to be conductor of the Boston Symphony Orchestra. When he invited a guest to conduct for his mid-season vacation, that person submitted his proposed program to Koussevitzky, and if any Tchaikovsky work was on it, it was removed. Only Koussevitzky himself could conduct Tchaikovsky with His Orchestra.

Once, in the mid-1940s, when Dimitri Mitropoulos was a guest conductor, Koussevitzky was infuriated with the performance and told him so. Mitropoulos was entirely different in his approach: more relaxed and less authoritarian in his attitude toward the orchestra and much less controlling of the dynamic range of sound than Koussevitzky. After the Friday afternoon concert, Koussevitzky left the first balcony where he had listened. Going down the backstage stairs as Mitropoulos was on his way up, Koussevitzky, his face livid, exploded, "Vot you have done to my orchestra? You made it sound like a brahss bahnd." Mitropoulos only smiled, yet his face turned red. I suspect that more words were spoken between them later in the Green Room. For Koussevitzky's remaining years with us, Mitropoulos never again appeared as guest conductor.

Koussevitzky's room was his retreat at all times, and its door was always closed. One did not ordinarily go there, or anywhere near, unless it was very, very important, or unless one was summoned.

*   *   *

He was not alone in his authoritarian image during the 1920s, 30s, and 40s. Leopold Stokowski of the Philadelphia Orchestra, and Arturo Toscanini with the New York Philharmonic were also sovereign maestros. Stokowski, originally an organist from England, went so far at one point as to refer to each person as "Number 25" or "Number 7," rather than by name or instrument.

Stokowski had begun his first season as conductor of the Philadelphia Orchestra with the arrogant attitude which character-ized his entire life in front of orchestras. Benjamin Kohon, former Philadelphia Orchestra bassoonist, wrote a letter, including a story about Anton Horner, longtime first horn player of the Philadelphia Orchestra, to Sol Schoenbach, principal bassoon-ist of the Philadelphia Orchestra in later years, and Schoenbach kindly shared the letter with me during the time I was editor of *The Horn Call.* "Aside from being a marvelous horn player, Horner stood up to Leopold Stokowski at times. . . . In his first season with the Philadelphia Orchestra (1912), Stokowski would always criticize the previous week's performances at the Mon-day morning rehearsal. After a few weeks of such harping at the men, Horner got up and told him to tell the orchestra about its good points, not only its faults. Stokowski never again made any remarks at Monday rehearsals." Nevertheless, Horner's no-tification that he was to move from first to third horn was con-tained in a letter put in his box at the Academy of Music before the season's first rehearsal, saying, in effect, "Your services as first horn are no longer required."

During my student days at The Curtis Institute of Music in Philadelphia, I had heard Stokowski from the school's box over-looking the stage at the Academy of Music. Although I reveled in the sound and perfection of the orchestra, I never enjoyed the show he was presenting to the audience as he stood on a high circular podium with, as I recall, three steps ascending to a throne-like affair. Meanwhile, a spotlight shown down from above on his carefully disheveled hair while he drew pictures in the air. No baton. Somehow the orchestra knew what he was doing and played. There are conductors who remain quite pro-saic with their gestures and demeanor in rehearsals but turn into acrobats and ballet dancers when the audience is behind them. But then, who doesn't know a concert-goer who says, "I am going to *see* Mr. X conduct tonight."

Stokowski and Koussevitzky had opposite ideas of orchestral sound, although both had, I believe, unusually wonderful ideas about what the symphony orchestra was capable of doing. Stokowski got a very opulent and thick, almost sensual sound from his orchestra, while Koussevitzky obtained a brilliant, intense sound. In Boston, we tuned to the pitch of A-444, but went higher as the instruments became warmer. This was much easier for the strings than it was for the winds. Our instruments are manufactured to a specific pitch, and only by "squeezing" could we get into the stratosphere where the strings had taken us. But it was brilliant—and beautiful.

Koussevitzky's rehearsals were many times more difficult to play than were his concerts. In fact, they were emotionally draining. Never were there only cursory readings, not even of the well-worn war horses such as the Brahms Second Symphony or the Leonore Overture No. 3. Every work, old as well as new, was approached as though for the first time, examined bit by bit, studied, honed, refined and polished until it shone. No matter what the piece was, Koussevitzky said of it that it "was the greatest of the greatest." No work he played was ever considered by him to be unworthy. Everything demanded the very best effort and playing. If, for example, the Brahms Second had been played sometime during the previous season and was brought out for a road trip in the following season, it was rehearsed and rehearsed as though for the first time. Nothing was left to chance for concerts. One could depend on Koussevitzky to conduct exactly as he had rehearsed. Some conductors have the idea of under-rehearsing and then looking for spontaneity at the concert. Intensity in a Koussevitzky rehearsal dominated every second of every breath and every bow. That was his spontaneity.

*　　*　　*

Composers who were having new works played by the Boston Symphony usually sat in the first balcony directly by the stage during rehearsals—only a few feet from Koussevitzky's podium. There were interchanges between the two as the conductor attempted to realize what the composer had written. However, it was usually the composer who was subservient to the conductor and to the way he decided the work should sound. Time after time, Aaron Copland would say, "Yes, Dr. Koussevitzky, it sounds better that way. I will change it in my score." But in the case of Bartok's *Concerto for Orchestra*, Koussevitzky had trouble throughout rehearsals, and concerts as well, with Bartok's irregular rhythms. Bartok, however, changed nothing.

Once, when Gretchaninoff was having one of his works premiered by Koussevitzky, he tried to change something which Koussevitzky was doing. Koussevitzky said to the orchestra, "Don't pay attention to him. He is a old man and don't know vot he vants."

Pierre Monteux said that no conductor should attempt to conduct without the score in front of him unless he knows and can remember every note of every instrument horizontally throughout the piece and every note of every instrument vertically throughout the piece. Some conductors are said to possess photographic memories of the score pages. I do not doubt that. But what I know is that too many do not produce much music from those pages—only notes. As Gustav Mahler said, there is much in music that is not written in the notes. The fad of not using a score at concerts was developed largely during my own memory from the late 1920s, onward, when Toscanini was coming into his element as a conductor in the United States and did not use a score in his concerts. There was a solid reason behind this: Toscanini had to have some roadmaps of the score in his mind, because his eyesight was becoming impaired, and he could not see anything without it being close to his eyes. Other conductors began imitating Toscanini and appeared without their scores as well. Some, in obvious theatrics, would have the score placed by the orchestral librarian on their desk, then walk to the podium, bow to the audience, turn to face the orchestra, and deliberately close the opened score. Koussevitzky always

had his score in front of him at concerts, and so did Sir Georg
Solti in Chicago. Other fine conductors are equally not averse
to using the score. Many more might benefit from its use.

Reiner said conducting cannot be taught: one learns to conduct only by conducting an orchestra. Yet classes and seminars
are given by established conductors to help aspiring young
musicians. Koussevitzky gave conducting classes when he opened
the Berkshire Music Center in 1940—but there was the student orchestra to serve as the guinea pig. At one time, Irving
Fine, who was a student of both composition and conducting,
was trying to conduct one of his own compositions with this
orchestra. Koussevitzky sat in the auditorium section of the
Music Shed near the stage, where he listened and watched his
conducting protegés. He would then come forward and talk to
them, voicing whatever criticism he might have. This particular conversation was to produce a quotation much used by members of the Boston Symphony. It was short and to the point:
"Fine, Fine, dot's awful."

Gregor Piatigorsky, virtuoso cellist, was soloist for a concert
on the West Coast which Monteux was to conduct. Because it
took place during the Second World War, the *Star Spangled
Banner* was to be played first, and Piatigorsky asked Monteux if
he might let his soloist conduct the national anthem. Monteux
agreed, and Piatigorsky took on his conducting task. When he
had finished and returned backstage, Monteux asked how it
had gone. Piatigorsky replied that it went fine and that conducting was very easy. Monteux replied: "Don't tell anybody."

THE INSTRUMENT

In Shakespeare's England the ancestor of our instrument was a tube of fixed length, perhaps similar to that shown in Figure 1. Its range would have been limited to the few notes of the overtone series, and its use would have been restricted to very simple signals such as the town's night watchman might have sounded during his rounds, or to signal a fire.

The *trompe de chasse* or *cor de chasse* was a long, slender hunting horn coiled in hoop form so that it could be carried over the shoulder. It almost certainly originated in France about the middle of the seventeenth century, in connection with an emerging,

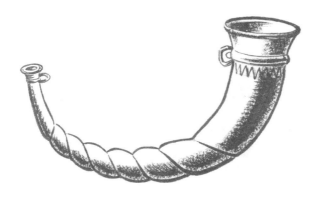

FIGURE 1. EARLY SIGNALLING HORN
Pen and ink drawing by Alex Grieve.

highly organized orchestra form. Its length was about seven feet three inches, and it was pitched in D, like the cavalry trumpet of that period (see Figure 2).

It must have reached England fairly soon, perhaps as early as 1667, and it was manufactured there and well known as the "French horn" before 1680. Before the turn of the seventeenth century it was being made in various sizes measuring between eight and sixteen feet. Handel's *Royal Fireworks Music*, first performed in 1749, was no doubt played on these hoop horns, because horns with crooks came to England as late as the 1730s and remained virtually unknown before the 1740s.

It is worth referring here to the fact that a pair of hunting horns appears in a detail from a painting at the Royal Theater in

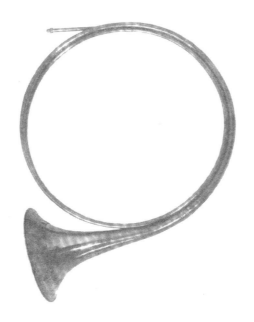

FIGURE 2. OPEN HOOP PARFORCE HORN, SINGLE COIL. *Circa seventeenth century.*

Turin (c. 1740), with bells lifted aloft over the heads of the players as they perform, accompanying action on the stage. Horns were often used in pairs, high and low, and this custom has prevailed to this day. Players usually specialize in one or the other register because of the unusually wide range of the horn, a range which, on the modern horn, extends to more than four octaves.

The introduction of the hunting horn for use indoors must have involved a rather raucous display of sound indeed. Because of its greater length, the hunting horn (Figure 3) had many

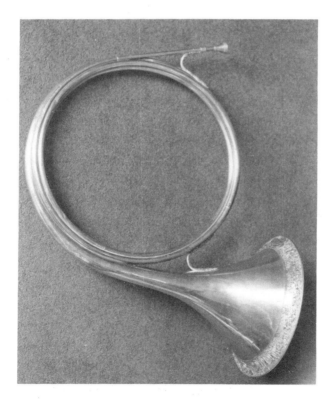

FIGURE 3. COR DE CHASSE IN D
WITH TWO AND A HALF COILS.

more overtones available than the horn of the night watchman. A favorite tonality for the hunting horn was the key of D. In 1680/81 the Bohemian Count von Sporck introduced the hunting horn into Germany, and it was taken up at once by the Nuremburg makers, the earliest known dated horn being a *Jagdhorn* (see Figure 4) in A by W. Haas (1682).

Apart from an elaborate series of hunting calls composed by Dampierre for Louis XV, many of which are still in use, music

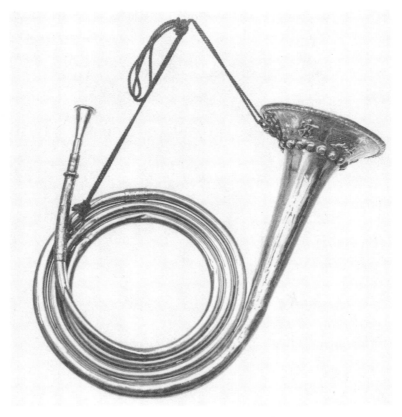

FIGURE 4. JAGDHORN IN D♭, 1688.
A later example from Johann Wilhelm Haas.

for the horn was not developed until the middle of the eighteenth century, when German players with instruments appropriate for orchestral playing were introduced to Paris, then representing the height of orchestral culture on the Continent. The Germans were the first to realize the musical possibilities of the horn and, in due course, to cultivate the lower register, though trumpet technique was the general practice during Bach's lifetime, when players "doubled" on trumpet and horn.

Reinhard Keiser's opera *Octavia*, produced in Hamburg in 1705, includes parts for two *cornes de chasse*. A separate horn was needed for each change of key. But this was obviated c. 1715 by the use of crooks—rings of tubing in assorted lengths, whereby the horn could be put into any key.

About mid-century, hand-stopping, i.e., partial closing of the bell with the hand, was introduced by Hampel in the orchestra of the King of Dresden. Thus the term "hand horn" was born. In Germany it was known as the *Inventionshorn*. Keeping the hand in the bell all the time, and using the hand to close the orifice more or less as required, not only allowed the production of a number of notes foreign to the harmonic series and the correction of harmonics out of tune with the tempered scale, but it also improved the tone. This conferred new status on the horn; it became a serious solo instrument in the hands of a number of virtuosi, nearly all of them of Teutonic or Slavic origin.

This instrument, the hand horn or Inventionshorn (Figure 5) was the one which Haydn, Mozart, Beethoven, Schumann, Brahms and Wagner had at their disposal. Wagner, in *Tannhäuser*, was still calling for a pair of hand horns while also scoring for a pair of valve horns. He had not yet fully accepted the new invention and was unwilling completely to let go of the old ways and sound of the hand horn. The horn had assumed by this time a smaller loop and was held with the bell pointing toward the floor.

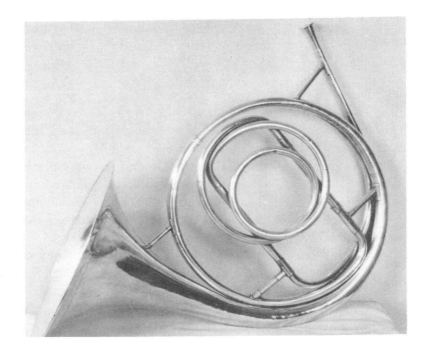

FIGURE 5. HAND HORN, OR INVENTIONSHORN
Paris 1823. Made by L. J. Raoux.

The valve which was to revolutionize all brass instruments was the invention of Heinrich Stölzel and Friedrich Blümel, patented in 1818. Shown in Figure 6 is the modern orchestral horn with rotary valves which conductors and audiences see in America today. This is the German model introduced to America by the many German horn players who came to this country in the late nineteenth and early twentieth centuries to fill positions in American orchestras. Its bore is wider than those of the old *cor-de-chasse* or of the hand horn, and it uses rotary valves.

In France, another type of valve was being developed with the perfection of the piston valve about 1839 by François Périnet

FIGURE 6. GERMAN HORN
Modern orchestral instrument in F and B♭.

(Figures 7 and 8). These valves are familiar to Americans as the type we see on trumpets. We do not usually find this French horn in American orchestras, although I was told that one of my colleagues in the Boston Symphony had used but given up his French horn sometime before I joined the orchestra in 1943. The sound of the French model is distinctly different from that

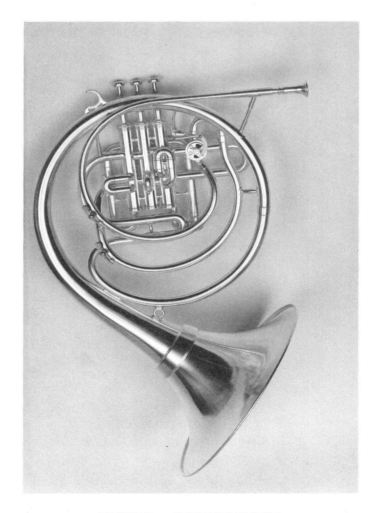

FIGURE 7. FRENCH HORN
Contemporary model by Selmer et Cie., Paris. In F and $B^\flat$, with 3rd valve ascending. Rear view.

of the German horn: more refined and smaller in volume. It is the instrument of Franck, Debussy and Ravel. Today, however, even French players are turning to the heavier, darker German instrument.

FIGURE 8. FRENCH HORN
Front view of Selmer double horn in F and B♭.
With 3rd valve ascending.

In Vienna there is yet another type of horn in use, generally known to us as the "Vienna horn," which employs a double pump-valve system. Its bore is different from both the German and French horns and its valve system is nearer to that of the French (see Figure 9). This horn possesses the "romantic" horn sound we associate with Schumann, Brahms and Bruckner, and is part of a tradition with which the Viennese simply will not part.

FIGURE 9. VIENNA HORN

Vienna Horn in F, showing long levers which pull out double pistons of each valve assembly when pressed by the fingers. Shorter tubing is furnished to put the instrument in B♭ alto. But it is not the same instantaneous system as that of the German double horn.

FROM THE SYMPHONIC REPERTOIRE

The excerpts discussed in the following were in a way chosen at random, in a way their choice dictated itself. While they are meant to reflect the horn player's standard repertoire, they obviously do so in a loose and selective manner. The choice was made with an awareness that standards change in time.

The same consideration holds for the occasional references to recordings. With the continuous immense proliferation of the recording market, what seems standard at a given time is antiquated within a generation. But the era of Koussevitzky, of Stokowski and Toscanini has remained more than a passing phase, and this is true to an ever so much greater extent of their repertoire. Thus the examples are representative of the orchestra's daily bread—a fare without which no orchestra players or conductors can enter into their profession. It is a fare which, we may fortunately say with confidence, will never be subjected to serious rationing or to oblivion.

Beethoven Symphony no. 3 ("Eroica") op. 55, Scherzo

This great passage has suffered from various insults. Beethoven wrote a straightforward and yet restrained fanfare for three balanced parts. Often sforzandos are heard as explosive attacks, rather than just as accents. Quarter notes are played staccato, rather than being given their full value. This may mar an otherwise good performance, especially through shortened notes at climaxes. In Böhm's recording with the Berlin Philharmonic, for instance, it becomes particularly noticeable (possibly through the fault of the recording engineer), because the eighth notes in the second horn part appear suddenly amplified. Many conductors slow down the tempo for this Trio, for instance Bruno Walter. Others place a grand pause before its beginning. Neither seems justified.

Beethoven Symphony no. 4 op. 60, Second Movement

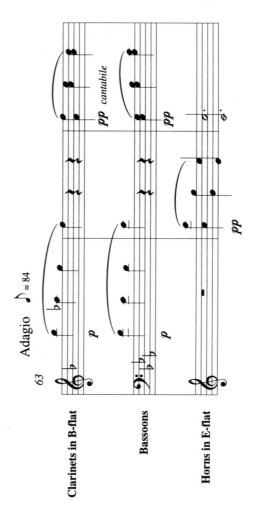

It is quite easy to play the clarinet so that it is scarcely audible. But a high C for horns in E-flat is difficult even in normal piano dynamics. The difficulty of the entrance is aggravated if the passage of the clarinets and bassoons is performed diminuendo (as is evident in Beecham's rendition in his recording with the London Philharmonic).

Beethoven Symphony no. 6 ("Pastoral") op. 68, V. Hirtengesang

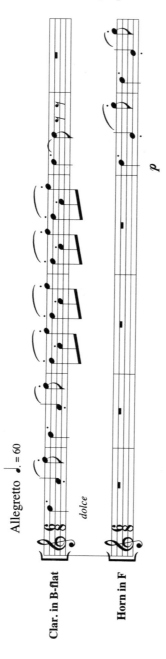

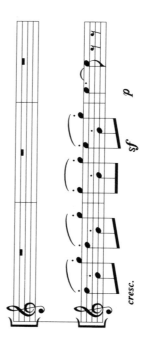

The non-legato of the clarinet must be matched by the horn. Too often conductors allow the horn to play this passage staccato, thereby destroying the continuous line. Recorded examples I have studied showed perfect executions by Carl Maria Giulini and the Philharmonia Orchestra, Bernard Haitink and the London Philharmonic Orchestra, and Paul Paray and the Detroit Symphony.

Beethoven Symphony No. 8 in F op. 93, Minuetto, Third Movement

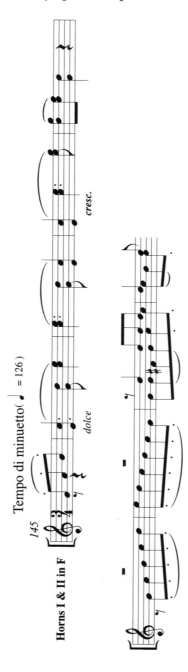

In the third movement of this work, it is a matter of phrasing that traditionally seems to stray from the composer's intentions. Some of the great conductors separate the opening four-measure phrase by short breaks after the first and second measures, so that the unity of the melodic line is lost. This becomes especially obvious when accompanied by crescendo and decrescendo emphasis—a sentimentalizing that distorts the simplicity of Beethoven's writing.

Following the second ending, the four-note motifs alternating between the two horns must maintain the same articulation and dynamic. *Subito piano* is truly sudden in the ninth bar after the second ending and must be strictly observed. Crescendo, back to piano, to crescendo again are essential to a correct performance. Legato continues until the eighth note staccato figures of bars 16 and 17; then the alternating motifs between the horns present the same problem of articulation and dynamics as that immediately following the second ending. These niceties of observing Beethoven's clear markings too often escape conductor and player alike. The diminuendo found in the last bars must be corresponding to that of the clarinet.

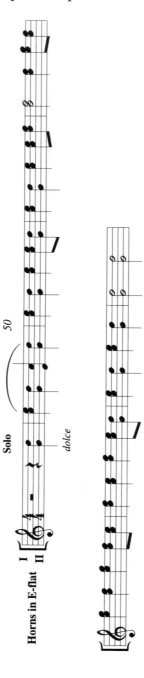

Beethoven Piano Concerto no. 5 op. 73 (Emperor), First Movement

This is one of the many passages in which the composer seems to have put an open question to the performer: are the measures following the first to be played in the same legato manner as shown in the beginning? This simple-appearing eight-bar phrase owes much of its proper execution to the piano solo which precedes it. There have been performances in which the eighth notes were even played staccato; but I have never heard any pianist who would render them in this manner. (Conductors must take care that each section of the orchestra performs its articulations in the same manner).

Beethoven "Fidelio." Leonora's aria, no. 9

Allegro con brio

Horns I, II, III in E

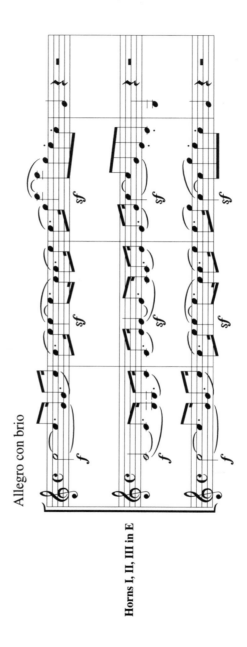

It is interesting that we have the testimony of Friedrich Gumpert, who became first horn player of Leipzig's Gewandhaus Orchestra in 1864 and whose legacy extends to American performers (including myself) through Anton Horner, first horn in the Philadelphia Orchestra, 1902-1946. He stated that by a tradition established at the Gewandhaus in Mendelssohn's days, this passage was always played detached throughout—not as written by Beethoven. The reason was that it was more powerful and safer on the hand horn then in use. The tradition was not broken until the modern valve horn appeared whose valves aid the player in making the slurs clean and safe.

Berlioz Symphonie Fantastique, op. 14, First Movement "Rêveries - Passions"

In measures 1 and 3 of this excerpt from the opening movement (*Rêveries*), each set of four notes is at times completely slurred. It does produce a smooth legato phrase. But Berlioz must have had a different idea in mind when placing the articulation marks as he did. It is interesting that he asked for accents on the thirty-second notes in measures 7 and 9; but to apply those in measures 1 and 3—as is occasionally done—merely destroys the line of the phrase.

I might add here that in the fourth movement of the work (the "Procession to the Stake"), the notation "1°" is entered in the score above the third horn—in accordance with the old custom of considering the second pair of horns consisting of a "first" and "second" horn. Another sort of confusion arose the first time Charles Munch rehearsed the overture to *Tannhäuser* with the Boston Symphony. He was quite visibly upset when the third and fourth horns did not play the opening solo. Their parts were written for a pair of natural horns in E—in France he had been used to such a pair playing those parts. But as "new" parts—re-written for the emerging valve-horn—they appeared now on the desks of the first and second horn players.

Berlioz Symphonie Fantastique, op. 14, Movement IV "Procession To the Stake"

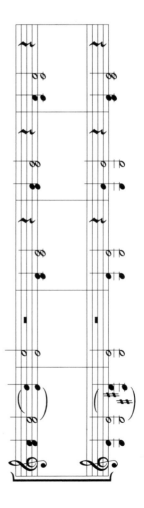

The score here referred to is that of the first edition by Schlesinger, Paris 1847. The second note is accented in each bar. Later scores have turned this accent into a diminuendo through careless printing, and some conductors adopt this misreading. Berlioz does not call for the removal of the mute until bar 62.

Of six conductors whose recordings I studied not one followed Berlioz's indications. Charles Dutoit, Paul Paray, George Solti, and Seiji Ozawa ignore the indication for the mute altogether. Sir Thomas Beecham renders these eleven bars muted, Jean Martinon merely the first four. Only Ozawa follows Berlioz's accents, all the others use a diminuendo instead, and the dynamic level ranges from pianissimo to mezzoforte.

Brahms Symphony no. 1 in c minor, op. 68, Fourth Movement

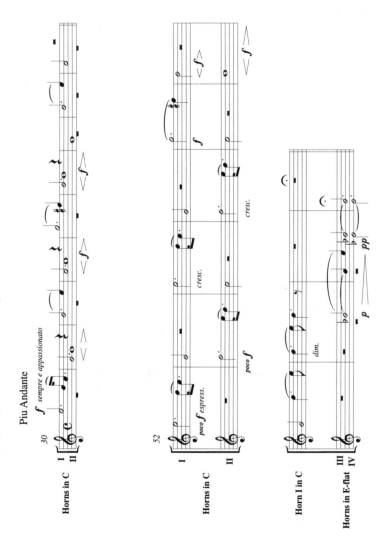

Of all the characteristic horn scoring contained in this symphony, none stands out quite as much as that in the last movement—the famous Alpenhorn Call which had originally been the composer's birthday greeting to Clara Schumann (*"Also blies das Alpenhorn"*—"Thus sounded the alp horn," September 12, 1868). It is a test of sustaining the melodic line. Help comes in the initial phrase from the second horn. But the balance of the two instruments must be perfect. All too often it is not—the flaw which Virgil Thomson laments (see page 7) and for which in the last analysis the conductor is responsible, because the players are less able to judge from their location.

Brahms Symphony no. 2, op. 73, Movement I

Allegro non troppo

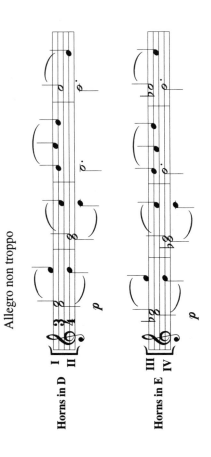

Singing fully sustained legato notes is a key to this opening. Bruno Walter was a master of such style. He was also the only conductor under whom I have played who insisted that the last quarter note of both first and third horns be kept dynamically strong, so that the line connects with the string phrase following.

Brahms Symphony no. 2, Movement 1

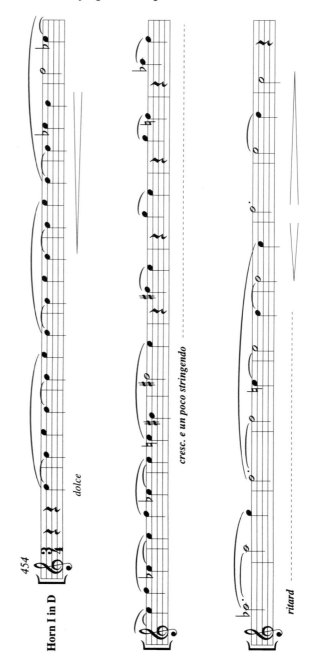

This solo can easily become sentimentalized if strict observance to crescendi and stringendo is not followed. Only *poco* stringendo is called for. Too many performances become almost hysterical in bars 12-15 because the stringendo begins earlier than indicated, and becomes excessive. Too much ritard in the last four bars causes an excess of Romanticism. George Szell's recording seemed to me actually one such performance. Kurt Masur and the Gewandhaus Orchestra give us a better example, in which the horn's beginning connects precisely with the trombone's ending note e', forming a continuous line. Phrasing can present a problem. However, I have found that a breath in bar eight after the first quarter, and again in bar twenty-one after the half note will produce the best result. If absolutely necessary the player can also take a breath in bar nineteen after the half note.

An amusing episode about this symphony and Sir Thomas Beecham occurred in Pittsburgh. At the week's first rehearsal he talked through the works to be played, canceling all rehearsals for the remainder of the week. Up shot a hand of a new and somewhat inexperienced young horn player who exclaimed, "but Sir Thomas, I have never played Brahms' second." Whereupon Beecham replied, "then you'll just love it when you play it at the concert."

Brahms Symphony no. 3, op. 90, Movement I

Allegro con brio

Horns I & II in C

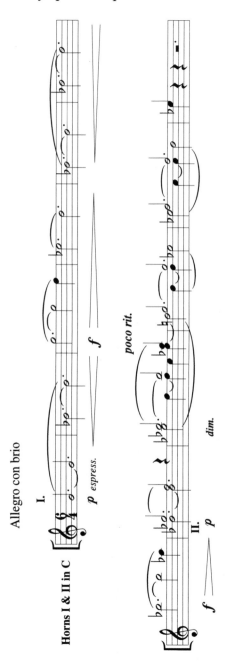

This passage, together with that following, from the third movement, is an excellent example of Brahms' deep understanding of the horn's lyrical sonority.

Intensity of tone should be the player's priority. It is especially important that the top note of each four-bar phrase not be overblown. Kurt Masur and the Gewandhaus Orchestra play the passage in its exact conception, the balance between the horns being accomplished by restraining the first horn, while allowing the second to dominate with the moving figure.

Brahms Symphony no. 3, op. 90, Third Movement

This phrase from the symphony's third movement (beginning at measure 98) is melodically continuous from the first to the last measure. There should be no break; but this is impossible for the wind instrument player. The composer's phrasing is conceived from the point of view of the pianist. We see his slurs across all notes of measures 8 and 9. But any player, no matter how skilled, must have ample reserve before approaching the climax in measure 9. A possible solution is offered by short breaks in measure 4 before the third beat, and in measure 8 before the second beat. (This is done in von Karajan's recording with the Berlin Philharmonic Orchestra.)

Brahms Symphony no. 4, op. 98, Movement II

Andante moderato

Horns III and IV in C

An unbroken melodic line is in order for these opening bars. That is easily accomplished, as the Boston Symphony and Charles Munch demonstrate in their recording, by staggering necessary breathing places between the two players. Focusing on a centered core of the forte dynamic will produce the necessary timbre.

Present-day concert goers are unlikely to agree with Hugo Wolf's appraisal of this symphony, appearing in Vienna's *Salonblatt,* January 24, 1886:

> "Conspicuous is the crab-like progress of Brahms' output. It has, to be sure, never reached beyond the level of mediocrity, but such nothingness, emptiness, and hypocrisy as prevails throughout the e minor symphony has not appeared in any previous work of Brahms in so alarming a manner. The art of composing without ideas has decidedly found in Brahms its worthiest representative. Just like the good Lord, Herr Brahms is a master at making something from nothing."[6]

---

[6]From *The Music Criticsm of Hugo Wolf,* translated, edited and annotated by Henry Pleasants (New York: Holmes & Meier, 1978). Copyright ©1979 by Henry Pleasants. Reproduced by the permission of the Publisher.

Brahms Variations on a Theme by Haydn, op. 56a, Variation VI

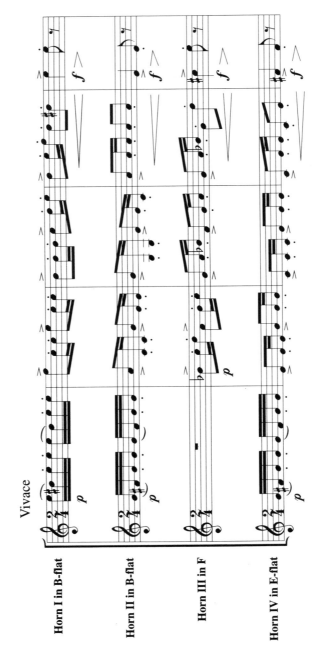

The composer's Vivace marking has been interpreted quite differently by various conductors. It is a fact concerning the acoustics of the horn that its sound experiences an ever so slight delay after it is initiated by the player. Because of this unalterable situation, the same passage performed by trumpets, for example, will always sound clearer at a fast tempo than when played on horns, and their slower response will need to be taken into account. Otto Klemperer and the Philharmonia Orchestra understood this acoustical problem well. They played moderato, insuring excellent articulation and dynamic contrasts.

Brahms Variations On a Theme by Haydn, op. 56a, Variation VII

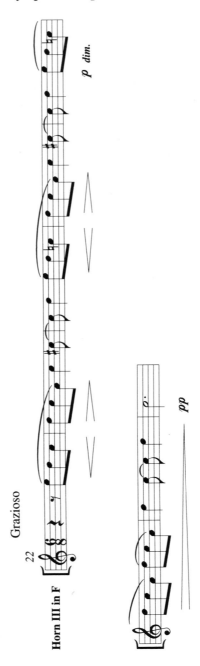

The dynamic level is determined by the preceding phrase. Conductors usually begin piano, although Kurt Masur, in his recording with the Gewandhaus Orchestra, goes to pianissimo. This allows the horn player to perform the passage in one breath, which, in turn produces a lovely flowing line. However, it is more usual to phrase the fourth bar by taking a breath after the fourth note, while still maintaining a good line. Sir Adrian Boult, in fact, demonstrates this with the London Philharmonic.

Brahms Piano Concerto no. 1, op. 15, Movement I
(Passage for both third and first horn using the same notation).

Maestoso - poco più moderato

Horns in F

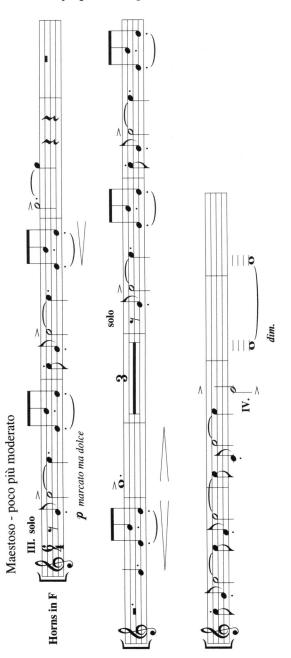

Correct articulation should follow that of the soloist. The third horn states the phrase first, followed later at bar 423 by the first horn in D. It is a serious error if the horns (third and first) play the non-legato notes staccato, as often happens. Brahms clearly indicates staccato notes when he wants them. Both horns should be in agreement on these points and conductors should see that they are. Accented notes should be in proportion to the dolce marking. There is an open question in the first horn's fifth bar as to whether or not the pianissimo marking called for in the score is a mistake. It does not appear in the otherwise exact dynamic markings of the third horn which the first horn mirrors. Players and conductors usually ignore this. Brahms' orchestration of the tutti seems not to have need for such a change.

My own memorable performance of this work was with Claudio Arrau and Koussevitzky, two great Romantics aptly paired. Koussevitzky tried to conduct the solos in two, but neither horn soloist could follow him. Finally, Arrau moved forward, and told him to conduct in six. Then all went as it should!

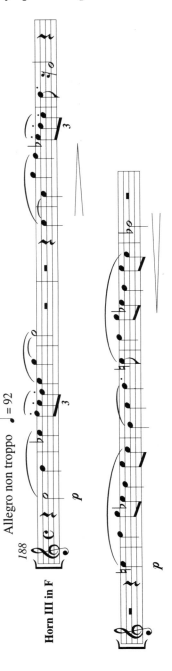

Brahms Piano Concerto no. 2, op. 83, Movement I

Allegro non troppo ♩ = 92

Horn III in F

This solo becomes more difficult if the conductor abandons Brahms' piano dynamic in favor of pianissimo. A problem in bars four to five becomes evident with Brahms' decrescendo to g" unless the beginning note c" is played dynamically stronger. Fortunately also, the stronger dynamics will project better into the auditorium than a pianissimo which tends to be covered by the piano soloist. A noteworthy recording has been left us by Claudio Abbado and Maurizio Pollini with the Vienna Philharmonic; my own best remembered performances are with Artur Rubinstein and Rudolf Serkin—they are different, but both ever so fine.

Chopin Piano Concerto no. 2 in F, op. 21, Finale, 112 measures before the end

N. B. The orchestra's notes are transposed here up a fifth, as they appear in the published horn parts.

The horn solo, beginning in the fourth measure of this excerpt, presents a challenge. The tempo of the movement is Allegro vivace, and its scherzo character is set by the piano soloist. Both tempo and character need to be maintained, and the dynamic of piano remains through all four measures. All of this is often ignored, and the passage prompted a memorable remark by Koussevitzky: "Please don't make me a *romance*."

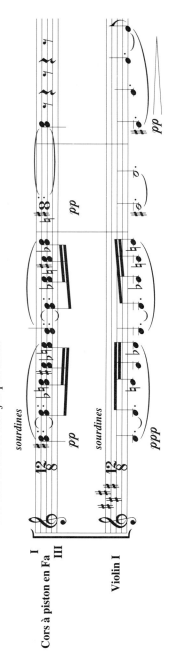

Debussy, Prelude "L'apres-midi d'un faune," 4 measures from the end

There are different kinds of mutes, and those conductors are indeed well advised who choose a muted sound with "sourdines" for Debussy's "cors á piston" in consultation with their players. It can result in a misty, cloudy effect of sonority that represents the perfect balance intended.

Debussy "La Mer," 1. From Dawn to Midday at Sea

Modéré, sans lenteur (dans un rhythme très souple) (♩ = 116)

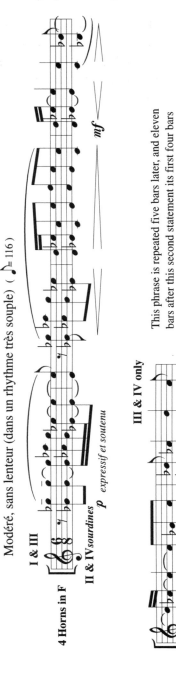

This phrase is repeated five bars later, and eleven bars after this second statement its first four bars reappear mezzoforte, with mute.

The dynamic level is piano, with mute, not forte with reliance on the mute to soften the sound. There is a great difference between these two approaches. It will usually make for a better balance when the lower voices are slightly stronger than the top, so that true octaves can be heard. Koussevitzky insisted on this, as well as on forceful forward drive without increasing the tempo.

In one of his guest appearances with the Boston Symphony during the Munch years, Pierre Monteux recounted to some of us his personal participation in the first rehearsal of *La Mer*. This was at the time when he was principal viola of Orchestre Colonne, Paris.

The musicians there didn't take Debussy's score very seriously, and became bored with it to the point that one of them made a paper boat which he pushed across the floor with his foot. The joke quickly caught on, and shortly a whole fleet of paper ships was sailing on the floor among men and instruments.

Debussy "La Mer," 2. Games of Waves

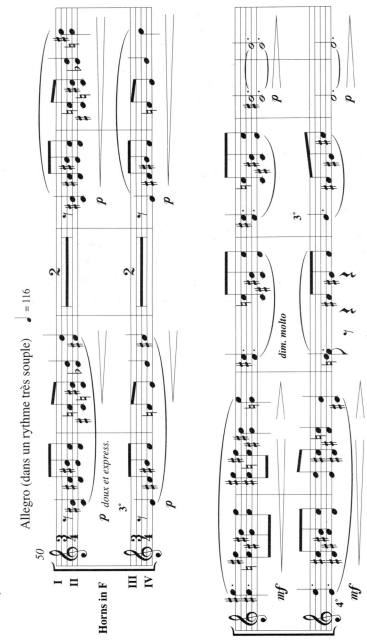

Problems of balance beset many conductors during this passage. Too often it is a first horn solo accompanied by some kind of indistinct rumbling from the other two players. If Debussy's dynamics are followed and the lower voices are brought out, a satisfactory balance can be obtained, and it is up to the conductor to do this. Players do not always know how their sound is projecting. Yet, some conductors tell the musicians that it is their problem, not his! The result is blame heaped on players—not where it belongs.

Debussy "Iberia" 1. Par les rues et les chemins

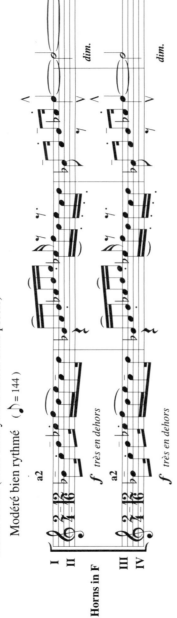

Debussy's articulations are not as easy to execute as it may first appear. Every eighth note is to be sustained for its full value, followed by a staccato sixteenth note. A careful conductor insists that the articulation remains Debussy's. In the Boston Symphony, under Charles Munch, a good line was maintained when all four horns played all the parts together; this avoids any delay in rhythm which might occur in the second and third bars.

Debussy "Iberia", 1. Par les rues et les chemins

The rehearsal numbers are those found in the Durand score.

Here the horns' articulation must match that of violas and cellos. Their individual lines must be equal in dynamics for proper balance (as is done by Pierre Boulez with the Cleveland Orchestra).

Debussy "Iberia," 2. Les Parfums de la nuit

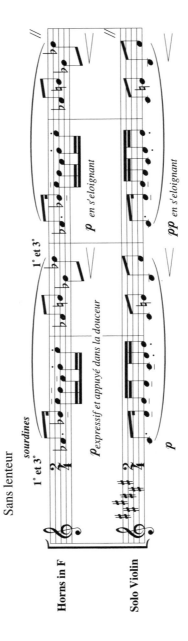

In this passage wonderful color of sound is obtained, because Debussy well understood the register of horns and violas when paired. The players, especially those of the horns, must produce a limpid tone and seek to produce sensuous inflection of articulation. It calls for the subtlety of the sensitive artist.

Dvorak Symphony no. 9, op. 95, "The New World," Finale

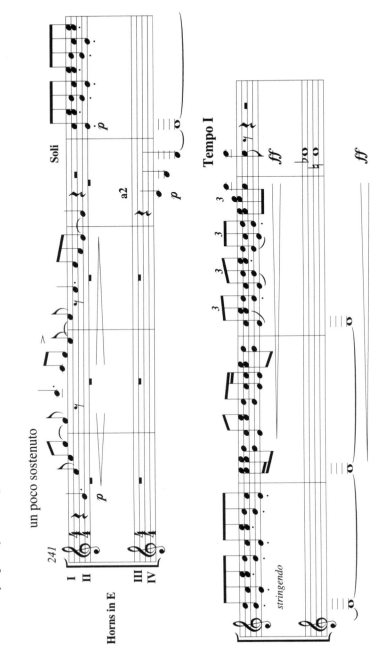

Louise Horner, elder daughter of the Philadelphia Orchestra's Anton Horner, relates the following story in connection with this passage: "The horns didn't please Ormandy, and he asked my father to rehearse the horn section." (Actually it was Ormandy who caused the problem because, in order to obtain greater brilliance, he was rushing the passage.) "My father rehearsed it as requested, but in 'tempo a la Horner,' and it was fine. Then he told 'his boys' (they were all his pupils): 'Now ignore Ormandy, and I'll talk to him.' He did talk to Ormandy and said: 'The accelerando is in the music. Just follow the horns.' 'Oh, Mr. Horner, I couldn't do that,' said Ormandy, to which my father replied: 'If you were accompanying a Heifetz or Horowitz, you would follow him . . . Just follow the horns.' They played, he followed, and all went well."

Haydn Symphony no. 51, Movement II

Adagio
I° solo

2 Horns in E-flat

This symphony, composed during Haydn's "Storm and Stress" period between 1771 and 1773, is a fine example of his writing in clarino-style. The players Johannes Thürrschmidt and Joseph Fritsch may still have been in service in the Esterházy court orchestra when this was written, though Thürrschmidt left the orchestra in 1772. Even if the symphony had not been composed before 1773, Haydn may well have had in mind the unusual cantabile style of playing by this pair of virtuosi. A highly skilled second horn player is required to play the last three measures, as is a first player, considering the extremely high register, particularly on the hand horn. Today's conductors leave it to their orchestra members to choose the instrument on which they can negotiate these parts (if the work is played at all), and probably are happy when all the notes are played. Neville Marriner, however, provides a splendid example of this work in his complete recorded cycle of Haydn's symphonies.

Mendelssohn, Symphony no. 4, op. 90, ("Italian") Third Movement

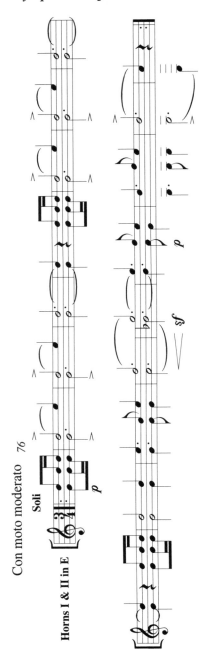

This solo passage, despite its simple appearance, presents a challenge to the players: it needs forward drive and force, even though it is soft and in a moderate tempo. This became especially apparent to me in listening to Munch's recording with the Boston Symphony, where it is beautiful but static. The impression is aggravated through a noticeable ritard in the last three measures—but Munch, in effect, tended to be a dreamer in conducting and sometimes allowed things to drift.

Mozart Symphony No. 40 K. 550, Menuetto

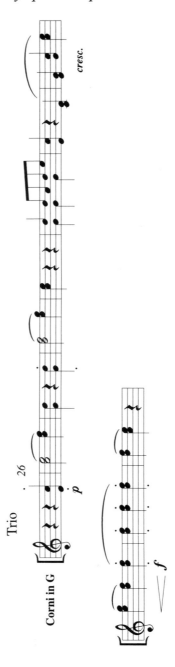

It has been interesting to hear this fine horn passage performed in Christopher Hogwood's recording with the Academy of Ancient Music on "authentic instruments" (hand-horns). It lies well within a comfortable range of the overtone series on the G horn (only f" needs to be altered by the hand to keep the phrase in tune). But one is apt to wonder how authentic the surprising crescendos are in measures 2 and 4, or the fast tempo (or the grace note, thrown in for good measure in bar 6, the second time around).

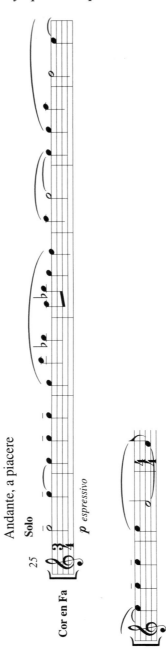

Ravel Piano Concerto in G, Movement I

Andante, a piacere

Solo

p espressivo

Cor en Fa

25

There is a recording of this work, with Ravel conducting (the orchestra is not named), and it shows the fast vibrato, in a piano dynamic range, which is typical of French players and which was likely intended by the composer. Performers often find the tessitura of this solo taxing, but it may merely reflect the psychological pressure before the actual entrance. The conductor who allows the player to relax and take over (without "conducting" the entrance) is well advised. Stravinsky has referred to Ravel as "an epicure and connoisseur of instrumental jewelry." This horn passage is one such jewel. Players of the German horn should keep in mind the lighter and smaller sound of the French instrument when performing this phrase.

The Boston Symphony invited Ravel to compose a work for its fiftieth anniversary (1931) and this concerto was that work.

Rimsky-Korsakoff, Capriccio Espagnol, op. 34

There is no dynamic marking in the score; conductors are free to choose it.

Stokowski, in his recording with the New Philharmonia Orchestra, is generally more conscientious about the articulation of this passage than other conductors. But he adds a conspicuous crescendo four measures from the end, which carries into the ensuing measure, and he has the last two measures played muted and heavily detached. Rimsky-Korsakoff was a master orchestrator and would surely have indicated an echo here, had he wanted one.

Schubert, Symphony no. 9 in C Major, First Movement

The famous opening phrase of this work, scored for two horns in unison, sets the stage for the entire first movement. Yet its simplicity is deceiving. The very first note presents a problem traditionally known. If the accented note is played too strong and loud, it is apt to have an effect upon the tempo—it is apt to slow the intended tempo to a plodding gait that turns out to be difficult to repair.

Schumann, Symphony no. 3, op. 97, ("The Rhenish") Second Movement

Schumann's orchestration has not infrequently come under critical discussion by orchestral musicians, and conductors have not been hesitant to rearrange his dynamics. The demands placed upon the horn players in the middle section of this movement represent a case in point. The phrase looks fine on paper, but the reality of a pianissimo in this register is suspect. I have heard no one who was able to carry it out, and it remains doubtful that anyone ever will.

Tchaikovsky Symphony no. 2, op. 17, Movement I

Andante sostenuto

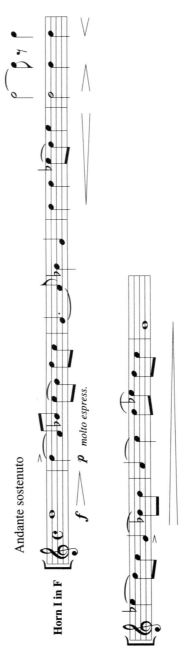

Horn "a cappella" sets both character and mood for the first movement. Its first note is like a declamation. Then the phrase proper commences, legato (and espressivo). Depending on the edition used, as noted opposite, one breathes in bar five usually after the half note, or the half-note tied to an eighth, as the case may be, and continues to the end without a break. If this is not possible for some players, a breath may be taken in the second bar from the end after the second quarter. Karajan and the Berlin Philharmonic demonstrate a perfect performance in their recording.

Symphonic Repertoire

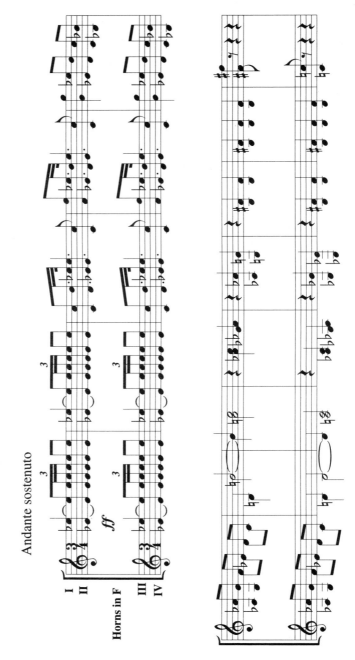

Tchaikovsky Symphony no. 4, op. 36, First Movement

Andante sostenuto

Koussevitzky's approach to the opening measures of this passage, performed with the Boston Symphony, was that of a Field Marshall commanding his troops. A brisk walk from the wings to the podium, shoulders erect, head held high, eagle-eyes riveted on each of the horn players (his troops), then a quick forward thrust with his baton as if bayonetting an enemy, and the fortissimo octaves sounded, while his second beat actually established the tempo. There was no preparatory beat. The short batons which he used (hand-made for him by the Orchestra's stage manager) were ample for the fervor and power with which he wielded them!

It is easy for horn players to overblow this opening. One must focus on the center of the tone and be aware that allowing it to spread ruins a fortissimo. The result is an ugly blast. In the large orchestras of the United States, six horns will generally be employed for this opening. But four will be used for the final five bars for a better effect of the decrescendo called for. Many conductors have the final bar played pianissimo for a beautiful effect.

Wagner, Siegfried Idyll

This famous work, written while the composer's son Siegfried was being born, uses the Siegfried theme from Wagner's music drama. Its articulation is most often ignored by players and conductors alike. The difficulty is that all notes must be given their full value: sustained but detached. It is not as great a difficulty as might appear at first glance, but the solo is nevertheless seldom performed in this manner.

Weber, "Der Freischütz", Overture

The opening of the work, nine measures before the entrance of the horns, is marked pianissimo, and there is no indication that this should change with the horn entrance. Gentle continuity of the melodic line is the prime requisite. It is better to lengthen, rather than to shorten the appoggiatura. The players' concern must be to maintain the singable and balanced character of the phrase, and no conductor can do that for them.

Care must be taken in bar six, so that the third horn's entrance and the first horn's last note are exactly in tune, and that the line connects with the same dynamic level in bar seven, where the first horn continues the melody. How cleverly the composer planned the tonality of each pair of horns in order for the harmonic series to work in his favor! In bar eight, following crescendo to mezzo-piano, the first horn's phrase continues uninterrupted through bar ten. If the conductor asks for more crescendo, it may be necessary to take a breath in bar eight, preferably after the dotted quarter note. Assuming that the conductor follows Weber's score, mezzo-piano will remain and a delicate accent can be made in the final bar. But how often do we hear forte instead, with a heavy and piercing accent more suitable to "Lützow's Wild Hunt."

Eugen Jochum and the Bavarian Radio Orchestra have left us an example of the ideal conception and performance in their recording of the complete opera.

EPILOGUE

The horn entered the modern musical scene as an orchestral instrument. The horn calls of the hunter, watchman and postilion were "solos" that only slowly found their counterpart in the classical repertoire. Bach's wonderful use of the instrument in the first Brandenburg Concerto and B Minor Mass, in the Christmas Oratorio and a number of his cantatas, forms lofty exceptions, as does Handel's use of it in the *Water Music* and some of his great vocal works. During the time of Viennese Classicism, the horn soloist Wenzel Stich made a name for himself (he liked to Italianize it as "Giovanni Punto"), and Beethoven wrote his Sonata Op. 17 for him.

Anton Horner (1877-1971) and Bruno Jaenicke (1887-1946) brought the finest traditions of horn playing from Europe and dominated two of the great American orchestras. Horner held the position of "solo horn" for most of his forty-four years (1902-1946) with the Philadelphia Orchestra and had been a pupil of Friedrich Gumpert of the Leipzig Conservatory. Jaenicke was one of the first horn players of the Boston Symphony Orchestra, beginning in 1913, as well as of the original New York Philharmonic, and when the Philharmonic merged with the Symphony Society of New York, remained there until 1943.

But Dennis Brain (1921-1957) blazed the trail as horn soloist for all who have since followed him. Solo appearances had been rare occasions in the United States, and they were not encouraged by the conductors, so that most of the twentieth-century horn players, up until the 1960s, held their place within the orchestra, not in front of it.

Brain burst onto the musical scene like a meteor. Not only were the great concertos, notably Mozart's, presented by him, but also the best of chamber music, all impeccably performed. Benjamin Britten's *Serenade* for tenor, horn and string orchestra, was written for Dennis Brain, and it stretched horn technique to limits unknown before. He was easy to know, and as easily approached by the eager youngster as by colleagues the world over.

The letter presented (opposite) and written to Gordon Grieve of Melbourne, Australia, illustrates his willingness to share in another's enthusiasm for the instrument. As one reads it, one becomes acquainted with the story of the French horn built by Raoux which Dennis Brain used in so many of his famous recordings—this is the true, the real *French* horn!

The photograph shows the French horn as belonging to Dennis Brain and which is mentioned in his letter to Gordon Grieve. (see opposite)

"Craigmore,"
37 Frognal, Hampstead, NW3
3rd February 1953

Dear Gordon,

Just a line to give you a few details of the instrument.

It was an hand horn with crooks made by Raoux, and which later had three detachable piston valves added, and in that form in F I made most of my recordings including the Strauss Concerto and Britten Serenade etc. There is an inscription on the uppermost flange of the bell. I then changed over to the B-flat horn and played for a while on a B-flat crook until I had it built into that key with one rotary valve for A and muting. Then, bearing in mind that the modern French players use an ascending third valve with good effect, I added another rotary, putting the whole instrument up into C alto and providing, in addition to very good high notes A, B, C, D, the pedal G and low G which features so much in the Schubert Octet.

One reason why I preferred it to the big German horn was the softer and more legato tone obtained, partly due to faster action and partly the quality of old, soft, metal. Now I use an Alexander B-flat with a narrow mouthpipe and small mouthpiece, which gives, I think, even better results though it is less easy to play so smoothly.

However I do not want to bore you with details, though if there is anything else you wish to know do not hesitate to drop me a line, and even though, as Tom will testify, I am a bad correspondent, I will eventually get round to replying!

With best wishes,
Yours Sincerely,

Dennis Brain

BIBLIOGRAPHY

Baines, Anthony, editor. *Musical Instruments Through the Ages.* Hammondsworth, 1961.

Brüchle, Bernhard, and Kurt Janetzky. *A Pictorial History of the Horn.* Tutzing, 1976.

Bush, Jerome. *Boston Symphony Orchestra.* Boston, 1936.

Crane, Robert, editor. *Symphony Orchestras in the United States.* Westport and London, 1986.

Endler, Franz. *Vienna: A Guide to its Music and Musicians.* Portland, Oregon, 1989.

Fitzpatrick, Horace. *The Horn and Horn Playing.* London, 1970.

Gregory, Robin. *The Horn.* London, 1961.

Howe, M. A. deWolfe. *The Boston Symphony Orchestra.* Boston and New York, 1931.

Jacob, Heinrich. *Anleitung zum Jagdhornblasen.* Hamburg, 1958.

Janetzky, Kurt, and Bernhard Brüchle. *The Horn.* London, 1988.

Langwill, Lindesay, Harold C. Hind, R. Morley-Pegge. *Waits, Wind Band, Horn.* London, 1952.

Morley-Pegge, R. *The French Horn.* London, 1960.

Pleasants, Henry. *The Music Criticism of Hugo Wolf.* New York, 1978.

Pratt, Waldo Selden. *The History of Music.* New York, 1930.

Schoenberg, Harold C. *The Glorious Ones.* New York, 1985.

Thomson, Virgil. *The Art of Judging Music.* New York, 1948.

Walter, Bruno. *Of Music and Music Making.* New York, 1961.